Milo
Is Not a Dog Today

Library of Congress Cataloging-in-Publication data is on file with the publisher.

Orginal edition © 2012 Coppenrath Verlag GmbH & Co. KG, Mü nster, Germany.
Original title: *Lullemu, wer bist DU?* (ISBN 978-3-649-61247-6). All rights reserved.
Text, pictures, and design by Kerstin Schoene and Nina Gunetsreiner
Published in 2014 by Albert Whitman & Company
ISBN 978-0-8075-4793-9
No part of this book may be reproduced or transmitted in any form or by any means,
electronic or mechanical, including photocopying, recording, or by any information storage
and retrieval system, without permission in writing from the publisher.

Printed in China.
10 9 8 7 6 5 4 3 2 1 NP 18 17 16 15 14

Cover design by Jenna Stempel

For more information about Albert Whitman & Company,
visit our web site at www.albertwhitman.com.

Milo
Is Not a Dog Today

Kerstin Schoene · Nina Gunetsreiner

Albert Whitman and Company
Chicago, Illinois

This is
Milo.

He loves to play and have fun.
Today he doesn't feel like
being a dog.

He would like to find a friend
to play with too.

So Milo begins his search...

"Will you play with me?"
Milo asks
the rooster.

"Look, I have feathers too!
Today I am a rooster!"
Milo crows back.

But the rooster just
laughs and struts away.

"Will you play with me?" Milo asks **the sheep.**

"But you are a dog!
I only play with sheep
who have

warm woolly coats like mine,"
she bleats.

"Look, I have a wool coat too! Today I am a sheep!" Milo bleats back.

But the sheep
just laughs and
strolls away.

"Will you play with me?"
Milo asks
the frog.

"But you are a dog! I only play
with frogs who have
floppy green flippers
like I do," she croaks.

"Look, I have floppy
green flippers too!
Today I am a frog!"
Milo croaks back.

But the frog just
laughs and leaps away.

"Will you play with me?"
Milo asks
the stag.

"But you are a dog! I only play with stags who have **strong pointy antlers** like mine," he roars.

"Look, I have antlers too!
Today I am
a stag!"
Milo roars back.

But the stag
just laughs and
stomps away.

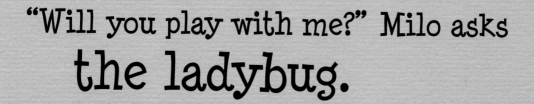

"Will you play with me?" Milo asks the ladybug.

"But you are a dog! I only play with ladybugs who have **delicate red wings** like I do," he buzzes.

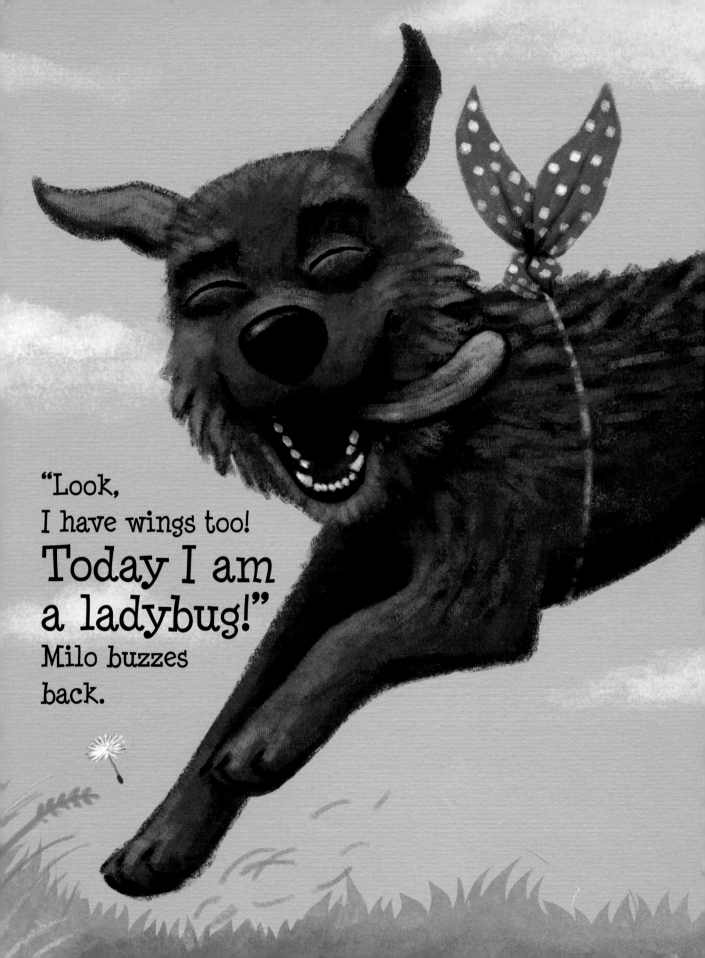

"Look,
I have wings too!
Today I am
a ladybug!"
Milo buzzes
back.

But the ladybug
just laughs and
flutters away.

But then **Milo the ladybug** meets Cleo the snail.

"I like your wings," Cleo says. "I'd love to be friends with a ladybug!"

"I like your shell," Milo says. "I'd love to be friends with a snail!"

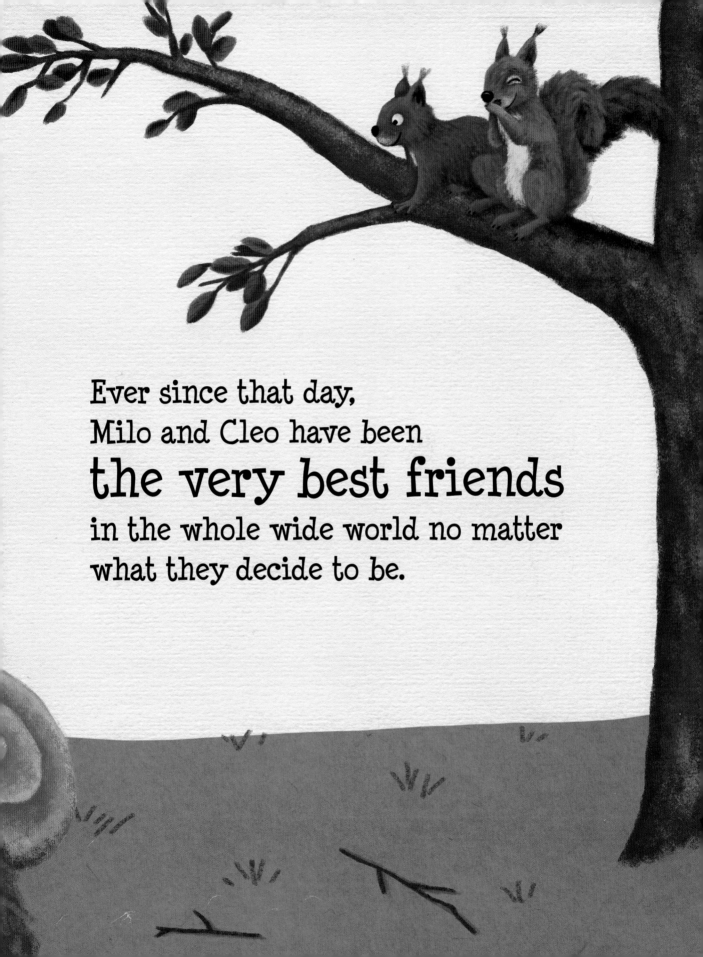

Ever since that day,
Milo and Cleo have been
the very best friends
in the whole wide world no matter
what they decide to be.